WHOSE NEST IS THIS?

by **HEIDI BEE ROEMER**
illustrated by **CONNIE MCLENNAN**

NorthWord
PUBLISHED BY TAYLOR TRADE PUBLISHING
Lanham • New York • Boulder • Toronto • Plymouth, UK

To Brandon and Colin, you've flown from the nest.
Forever and always—You are the BEST!
—H. R.

To Geoff, who built our nest.
—C. M.

The text and display type were set in Shannon and Atlas
Composed in the United States of America
Edited by Lois A. Rainwater
Designed by Pamela Darcy of Neo9 Design Inc.

NorthWord

BOOKS FOR YOUNG READERS

Published by Taylor Trade Publishing
An imprint of The Rowman & Littlefield Publishing Group, Inc.
4501 Forbes Boulevard, Suite 200, Lanham, Maryland 20706
www.rlpgtrade.com

Estover Road, Plymouth PL6 7PY, United Kingdom

Distributed by NATIONAL BOOK REVIEW

Library of Congress Cataloging-in-Publication Data
Roemer, Heidi.
Whose nest is this? / by Heidi Bee Roemer ; illustrated by Connie McLennan.
p. cm.
ISBN 1-58979-386-2 (hc : alk. paper)
1. Birds—Nests—Juvenile literature. 2. Animals—Habitations—Juvenile literature.
3. Nests–Juvenile literature. I. McLennan, Connie, ill. II. Title.
QL675.R59 2009
591.56'4–dc22   2007021870

∞™ The paper used in this publication meets the minimum requirements of American
National Standard for Information Sciences—Permanence of Paper for Printed Library
Materials, ANSI/NISO Z39.48-1992.

Printed in China.

Springtime is here. There is work to be done
as animal parents make nests for their young.
Using pebbles or woodchips, even mud, spit, and leaves—
many creatures make nests. . . . Whose nests are these?

A walnut-sized nest rests high in a tree.
Its two pea-sized eggs are a wonder to see!
Fashioned with spider silk, leaves, and green moss,
this nest lined with plant fluff is velvety soft.

Whose nest is this?

A hummingbird's nest

Blobs of mud, gobs of mud, dry hard and stiff.

These spit-and-mud structures are cemented to cliffs.

Hear hungry young chicks as they *cheep-cheep* inside.

Hundreds of huts dot the rocky hillside.

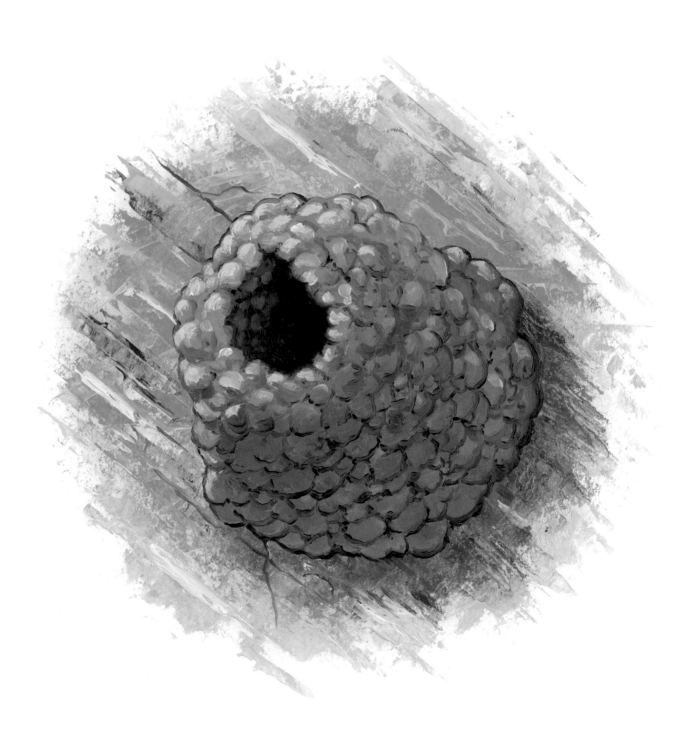

Whose nest is this?

A cliff swallow's nest

With a flick of her flippers, she clears the debris
and digs out a pit in the sand by the sea.
She lays leathery eggs (a hundred or so!)
and buries them all in a deep sandy hole.

Whose nest is this?

A sea turtle's nest

Snuggled near reeds in a wet marshy spot,
this nest keeps the eggs warm as it starts to rot.
Anchored securely, it's just like a boat—
The odd bowl-shaped nest is constructed to float!

Whose nest is this?

An eared grebe's nest

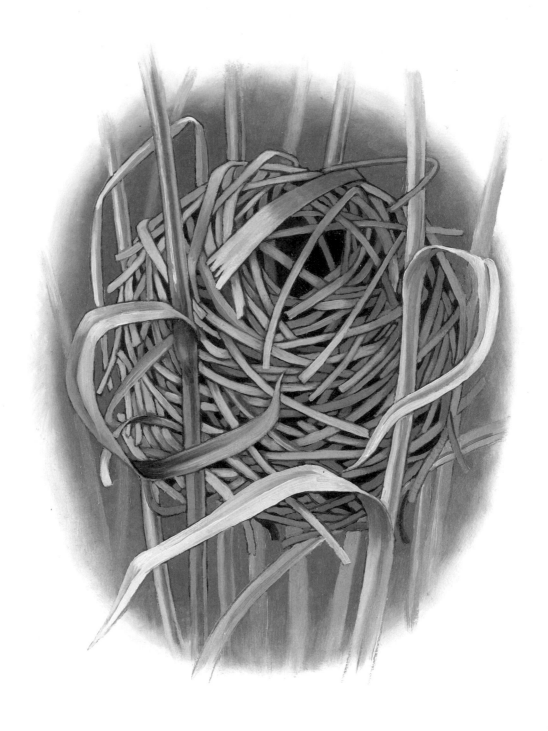

Bending green stems, he chews and he weaves.

He limberly climbs on his aerial trapeze.

With delicate paws and sharp little teeth,

he crafts a grass nest slung from tall stalks of wheat.

Whose nest is this?

A harvest mouse's nest

A chalky white egg, only one, rests alone
on a towering mud-mound that's shaped like a cone.
Thousands of chicks crowd the banks of the shore.
And when this egg hatches, there will be one more!

Whose nest is this?

A Caribbean flamingo's nest

This nest-building male tries so hard to please.

His nest is decked out with hair ribbons and keys,

flowers, caps, berries—most items are blue.

He's hoping a female will say, "Yes, I do!"

Whose nest is this?

A bowerbird's nest

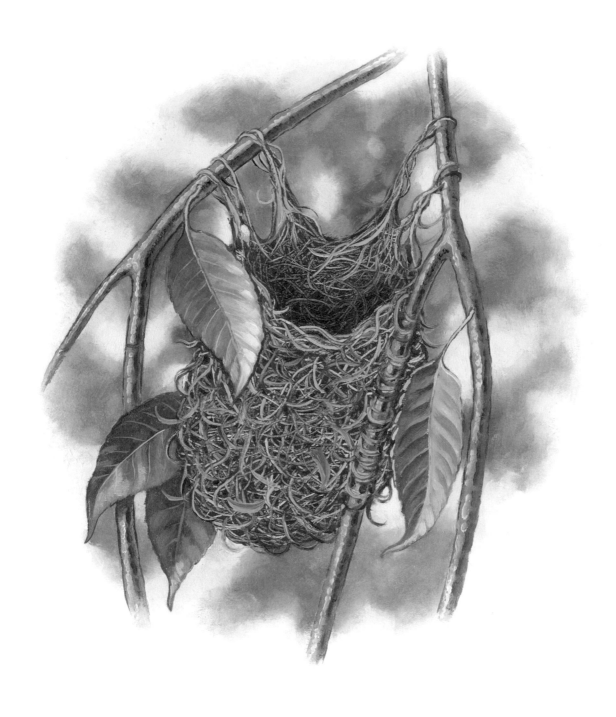

Long strips of bark, tough grasses, and vines
are wrapped 'round a branch like pieces of twine.
Hung from a limb, the pouch sways in the breeze
and rocks like a cradle high in the trees.

Whose nest is this?

A Baltimore oriole's nest

A hard-working papa, he won't stop to rest.
With bits of green algae, he forms a fluffed nest.
To hold it together, what does he do?
His body produces a waterproof "glue."

Whose nest is this?

A three-spined stickleback's nest

Imagine a rocky-hard "nest." Can that be?

Picture an egg balanced delicately.

High on a cliff this egg rests on a ledge.

Whew! It rolls in a circle—not off the edge.

Whose nest is this?

A common murre's nest

She snatches up plants with her terrible teeth
and piles the foliage in a ten-foot-wide heap.
Her eggs incubate in this super-sized thatch.
One day in late August, wee reptiles will hatch.

Whose nest is this?

An alligator's nest

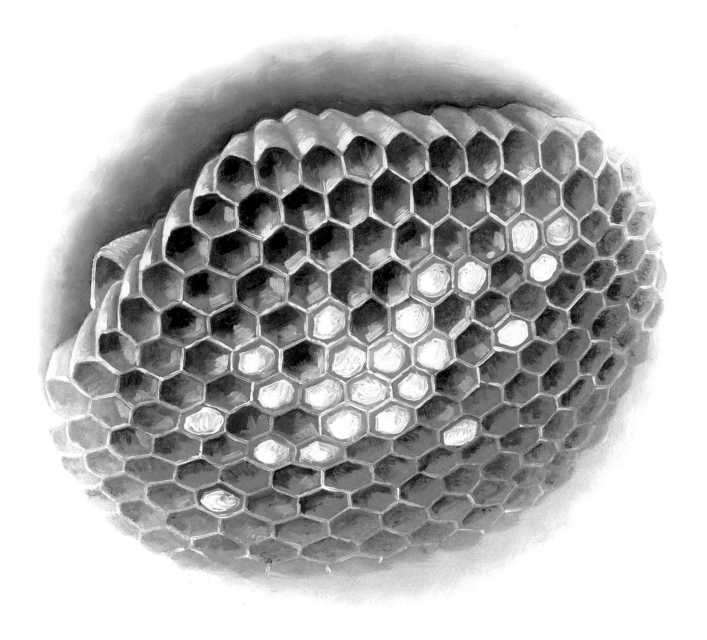

A papery palace that's fit for a queen,
it's unlike most nests you have probably seen.
Each nursery chamber has six-sided walls.
One egg rests in each—there are hundreds in all.

Whose nest is this?

A paper wasp's nest or hive

A woodpecker lived here, but not anymore.
The new owner moved in and she's guarding the door.
A giant Saguaro makes quite a fine home
for a bird that's too lazy to build one of her own.

Whose nest is this?

An elf owl's nest

There are mammals and reptiles and insects who nest.
Birds, too, build unique nests that suit them the best.
Some nests provide shelter, and some are for show,
but the best nests are those in which young babies grow!

Fun-Fact Glossary

Ruby-throated Hummingbird
This busy little female builds a nest, incubates her eggs, and feeds her young without any help from her mate. The mother protects her babies from predators such as hawks, other birds, and even large hungry insects!

Cliff Swallow
Swallows cluster together in colonies. Mated pairs nest on rocky cliffs or under the shelter of bridges. Each couple carries about 1,000 mud pellets to create their mud nests. A female may lay her eggs in her own nest or in a neighbor's nest.

Sea Turtle
When she is about 30 years old, a female sea turtle is ready to mate. Once she lays her eggs on the beach, her parenting job is done and she heads back to sea. After incubating for about two months, the baby turtles hatch, dig their way out, and race toward the ocean, trying to avoid predators along the way.

Eared Grebe
As the grebe's floating nest rots, it provides warmth that helps incubate the eggs. Though grebes don't fly well, they certainly can swim! The chicks are able to swim soon after hatching, but for the first few weeks they prefer to be carried around on their parents' backs.

Harvest Mouse
Baby mice are blind at birth and completely dependent on their mother. But in less than two weeks they begin exploring outside the nest. When they are 16 days old, the rowdy youngsters are able to take care of themselves.

Caribbean Flamingo
Flamingo parents share nest-building, egg-sitting, and baby-feeding duties. Two weeks after the chick hatches, it joins other chicks in a huge group called a crèche. The crèche is like a large nursery. Amazingly, parents are able to single out their own chick on the crowded shores.

Satin Bowerbird
Hoping to impress a female, the male decorates his bower "nest" site with care. If the female is pleased with his efforts, she will mate with him. Then the female builds her own shallow, saucer-shaped nest in a nearby tree or bush where she lays one to three eggs.

Baltimore Oriole
This cheery songbird typically lays four to six eggs in a flexible, waterproof pouch. The chicks hatch after only two weeks and are fed and guarded by both parents. Orioles eat caterpillars, insects, fruits, and berries. They are likely to visit feeders stocked with orange wedges, nectars, or peanut butter.

Threespine Stickleback Fish
When the male stickleback's barrel-shaped nest is finished, one or more females deposit their eggs inside. The male fertilizes the eggs and guards the nest for six to ten days. He continues to protect his fry, or baby fish, until they can care for themselves.

Common Murre
These seabirds are superb swimmers and fast flyers. They come ashore only to breed. Three weeks after hatching, juveniles leap off high cliffs with stubby, half-grown wings and glide out to sea. They remain with their parents until they are about two months old.

American Alligator
Baby alligators use an egg tooth to crack open their eggs. When the mother hears their soft grunts, she helps dig them out of the nest. The yellow-and-black striped hatchlings are 6 to 8 inches long. Young gators stay with their mothers for 18 months.

Paper Wasp
Paper wasps usually don't attack unless their nest is disturbed. A wasp sting is painful and the venom can be deadly for some people. Only the female is equipped with a "stinger." Wasps secrete another chemical that they spread around the base of their nest to keep hungry ants away from their eggs.

Elf Owl
The male's mating song, a high-pitched "whi-whi-whi-whi-whi," is a familiar nighttime sound in the southwest United States. In spring, the female lays three eggs, which hatch in 24 days. Only 5 to 6 inches long, the elf owl is one of the tiniest owls in the world. If captured, the owl goes limp and pretends it is dead until the danger has passed.

As a freckle-faced tomboy, HEIDI BEE ROEMER loved nothing better than to snuggle in the arms of an old willow tree with a good book. These days the author of *Come to My Party* and *What Kinds of Seeds are These?* enjoys helping other writers hone their word-crafting skills. She conducts workshops for children and adults and is also an instructor for the Institute of Children's Literature. Heidi and her husband, Ric, recently became empty nesters when their sons, Brandon and Colin, flew the coop. For more information, visit www.HeidiBRoemer.com.

CONNIE MCLENNAN worked in advertising and editorial illustration for many years before turning her attention to the children's market. *Whose Nest Is This?* is her ninth illustrated children's book. She works in her studio at home in Rocklin, California, where she lives with her husband, teenage son, and one big, black cat.